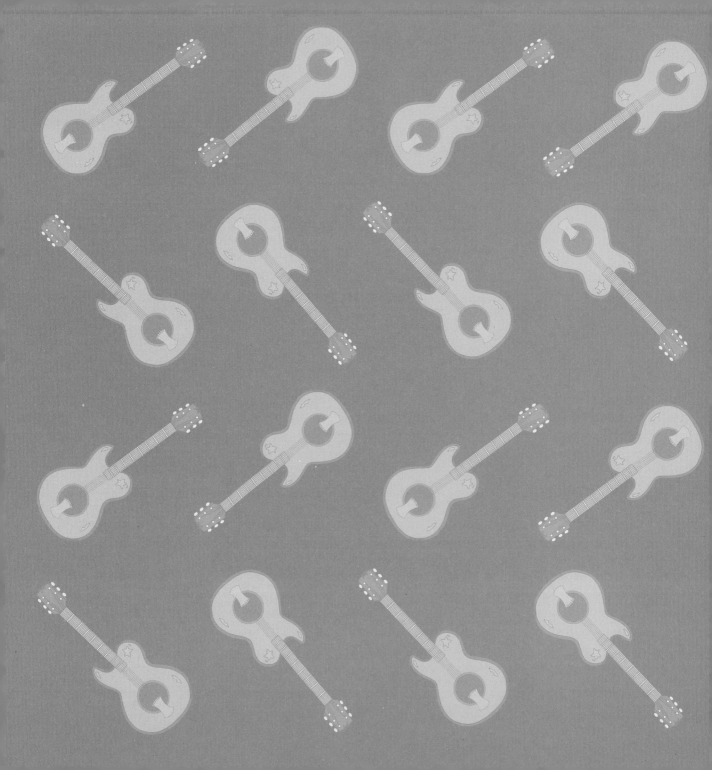

Harvest Hoedown

Adaptation by Gina Gold
Based on the TV series teleplay written by Lazar Saric

Houghton Mifflin Harcourt
Boston   New York

For information about permission to reproduce selections from this book, write to Permissions, Houghton Mifflin Harcourt Publishing Company, 3 Park Avenue, 19th Floor, New York, New York, 10016.

ISBN: 978-1-328-69596-3 paper over board
ISBN: 978-1-328-69597-0 paperback
Design by Lauren Pettapiece
Cover art adaptation by Artful Doodlers Ltd.
www.hmhco.com
Printed in China
SCP 10 9 8 7 6 5 4 3 2 1
4500654535

It was a special day in the country. The Renkinses had invited everyone to a hoedown at their barn to celebrate the harvest. George wasn't sure what a hoedown was, but getting ready for one sure was fun!

Mr. Renkins was explaining to George and his friend Allie that a hoedown was a big party with hayrides and square dancing. "And the best part is the live bluegrass music!" he added. "Bluegrass is lightning-fast, foot-stompin' music that'll make you want to jig. It's a hoot!" Mr. Renkins said with a laugh.

Suddenly, George and Allie heard music in the distance. Everyone ran outside and saw a double-decker bus pulling up to the barn. There were musicians on the top deck! Mrs. Renkins introduced the group as the Uptown Bluegrass Band.

George had never seen so many instruments before. There was a banjo, a fiddle, an upright bass, and a mandolin. And the very last instrument was a guitar, played by a man named Jerry. The guitar looked like the most fun to play!

George and Allie ooh-ed and ahh-ed over Jerry's dazzling guitar.
"You like my guitar?" Jerry asked. "I made it myself." George and Allie were
amazed. "It was easy," Jerry said. "Anyone can make a guitar if you have
the right parts."

"I used to play the bluegrass guitar too," the man with the yellow hat said. Jerry invited him to play with the band at the hoedown. But the man wasn't sure. Besides, he'd left his guitar at home. "George and I will go get your guitar!" Allie said. And they ran off toward the house.

Back at the house, George found his friend's guitar. He brought it outside to show Allie. But it was covered in dust.

"Let's give it a bath!" Allie said. "Grandma says there's nothing like a bath to make you bright and shiny!" So George and Allie put the guitar in the tub and gave it a good scrub.

"Uh-oh," Allie said as she looked at the soggy instrument. The bath hadn't made the guitar shiny at all. It made it lumpy and peely.

George needed another guitar for the man to play at the hoedown, and fast! Then he remembered what Jerry had said: "Anyone can make a guitar. You just need the right parts." George knew just what to do. He'd make a new one!

The first thing George and Allie needed was a box with a hole in it just like a guitar. First they tried a shoebox, then a crayon box. But both were flimsy and didn't have holes. The tissue box cover had a hole, but there was no back.

Then George saw something that looked perfect. A birdhouse! It had a hole and it was very sturdy.

"Now we need something long and wooden to put strings on," Allie said. So she searched the house and came back with a spoon with a long handle. But it was too skinny. Next, they tried a paper towel tube. But it unraveled. Nothing was working!

George was getting worn out, so he sat down on the floor to think. He looked around and realized . . . this tennis racket was perfect!

Finally, George's instrument was starting to look like his friend's guitar . . . except it needed bumps on the long wooden part. Chopsticks would do the trick! George glued some onto the tennis racket and waited for them to dry.

Next, George and Allie needed guitar strings. Allie found a basket full of things that might work. There were shoestrings, a yo-yo string, some fishing line, a picture wire, and a rubber band. George couldn't decide which to use, so he used them all!

George and Allie were almost done, but they still needed a way to attach the strings to the top of their guitar. George noticed that the picture wire he'd found earlier was attached to a frame by hardware that turned—just like the pegs on the man's guitar. They were perfect!

George was proud of his new guitar. It looked great!

Just then, the man with the yellow hat came home with Jerry. When the man saw his soggy guitar, he couldn't believe his eyes. "What happened?" he asked. "Don't worry, Mr. Yellow Pants," Allie said. "You can still play tonight. We made you a new guitar!"

"This is great!" Jerry said. "Bluegrass music has a tradition of using found objects like washboards and spoons. No one's ever seen an instrument like this! It's a shoestring, fishing line, yo-yo, picture wire, tennis racket, birdhouse, rubber-band-o-lin!" George and Allie giggled.

That night, everyone arrived for the hoedown. George's friend joined the band and played his new instrument.

Folks danced and sang and had a great time—especially George and Allie,
who got to play the washboard and spoons! It was a hoot!

Make a String Instrument

George and Allie learned that many bluegrass instruments are made from found objects, so they built a guitar out of the things they found. Can you make an instrument out of things from your house?

You'll need . . .
- Empty containers like a plastic wash basin, a large foil roasting pan, the bottom of a food storage container (without a lid), or an empty coffee can.
- Big rubber bands of different widths—thick, medium, and thin.

What to do:
1. Take three or four rubber bands of different widths and wrap them around a container. The rubber bands shouldn't be so tight that they don't fit around the container or so loose that they fall off. Just a little loose.
2. Pluck each rubber band with your finger. Try strumming them all at once.
3. Listen to the different sounds—or pitches—the rubber bands make. Do you hear a high pitch or low pitch?
4. Which rubber bands make high sounds? Which ones make low sounds? Are these the skinny ones or wide ones?
5. Add one more rubber band to your instrument. Based on the sounds you've already heard, can you guess what kind of pitch the new rubber band will make? Will it be higher or lower than the sounds you've already made? Or maybe in between?
6. Experiment with large and small containers. Does the size of the container make a difference? Does the material that the container is made of matter? Listen carefully.

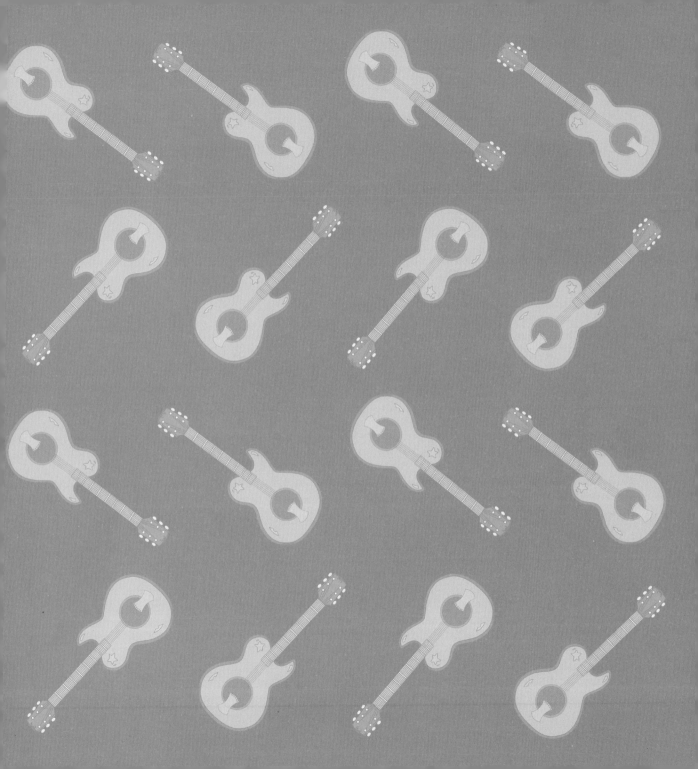